The Shu Monster

Written by Kathy Webb

Illustrated by Fabrizio Di Baldo

Collins

The Monster Carnival was a very busy place.
Dot felt unsure. It was unusually loud and a bit too crowded.

She found a space to sit quietly and watch the other monsters on the climbing wall.

"Come and play," said Macy.

"It'll be fun," said Lucian.

But Dot was still unsure. "No, thank you," she said.

3

Dot wished she could climb with the others, but her tummy was tied up in knots and she felt too small.

Dot knew she should be brave and say "yes" when they asked her to play, but what if she got the game wrong? They might not play with her again.

Help!

So she stayed in her safe place.
Dot enjoyed watching all the action at the carnival.

She giggled at the monsters having a race, knocking over the cans and bouncing on the bouncy fort.

Maybe *not* joining in could be fun, too.

Macy and Lucian came and sat with Dot in her special place.
"Do you want to play?" said Macy.

"Come on," said Lucian, with a big smile on his face. "It'll be fun."

Dot was still unsure.

"No, thank you," she said.

Dot watched Lucian and Macy play with the ball.

Until ...

"Oh no!" cried Lucian. "Now what are we going to do?"

The ball had rolled into a tiny space behind the ice-cream stall.

Lucian and Macy ran over to Dot.

"Please can you help us?" asked Macy. "We knocked the ball behind the ice-cream stall."

"You are small, Dot. Can you reach it for us?" asked Lucian.

Dot wasn't sure what to do. What if she couldn't reach the ball? What if she got stuck behind the ice-cream stall?

Dot wanted to be helpful, so she got down on her hands and knees and peered into the darkness.

Dot knew she had to be brave ... so she wriggled into the tiny space.

She felt the ball with the tips of her fingers, then quickly grabbed it and crawled out.

Dot was glad to be back in the sunshine.

"Hooray!" Lucian cheered, giving Dot a pat on the back.

"We knew you could do it," said Macy. "Thank you for helping us."

Dot smiled shyly.

"We're going on the bouncy fort," said Lucian. "Do you want to come?"

Dot was feeling brave. "Yes, please," she said.

Dot bounced ... and climbed ... and raced.

She was enjoying herself too much to feel unsure about anything.

After all the action and fun, Dot needed a rest. She found her special place and sat quietly.

Dot still feels unsure sometimes. But when Macy and Lucian ask her to play, she often says, "Yes, please." Sometimes she says, "No, thank you," and then she sits happily by herself, watching the other monsters.

And that is fun too.

A brave monster

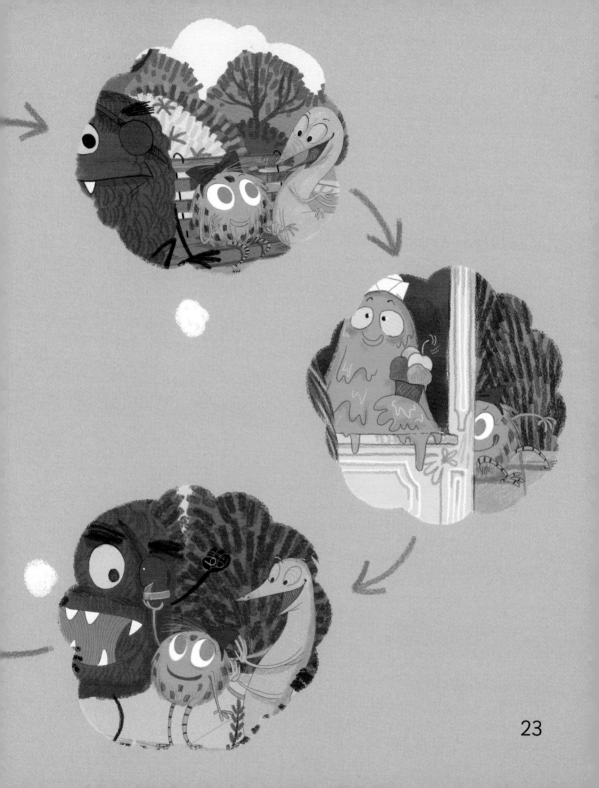

After reading

Letters and Sounds: Phases 5–6

Word count: 470

Focus phonemes: /n/ kn /m/ mb /r/ wr /s/ c, ce /zh/ s /sh/ ti, ci, s

Common exception words: of, to, the, into, are, said, do, oh, says, busy, anything

Curriculum links: PSHE

National Curriculum learning objectives: Reading/word reading: apply phonic knowledge and skills as the route to decode words, read common exception words, noting unusual correspondences between spelling and sound and where these occur in the word; read other words of more than one syllable that contain taught GPCs; Reading/comprehension: develop pleasure in reading, motivation to read, vocabulary and understanding by being encouraged to link what they read or hear to their own experiences

Developing fluency

- Your child may enjoy hearing you read the book.
- Take turns to read a page of the main text, encouraging the use of different voices for each character.

Phonic practice

- Challenge your child to identify the /s/ or /sh/ sounds in each of these words:

  Macy   space   special   action   bouncing   sure

- Challenge them to think of other words containing the /s/ sound but spelt with the letter "c". They could think of words that rhyme with **space** and **ice**. (e.g. *race, face, pace, lace; lice, nice, twice*)

Extending vocabulary

- Point to **shy** on the cover and ask your child to suggest a synonym. (e.g. *nervous, unsure, uncertain, timid, scared*) Repeat for **brave** on page 17. (e.g. *courageous, heroic, daring, fearless*)
- Take turns to point to a word and challenge each other to suggest a synonym.

Comprehension

- Turn to pages 22 and 23. Challenge your child to tell the story as if they were Dot, beginning, for example, "The Monster Carnival was very noisy and I felt unsure."
- Ask them to use the pictures as prompts for each event and how they felt.